OUR GOD IS BIGGER THAN THAT!

Michelle Medlock Adams
and Eva Marie Everson

Illustrated by
Anna Jones

END GAME Press

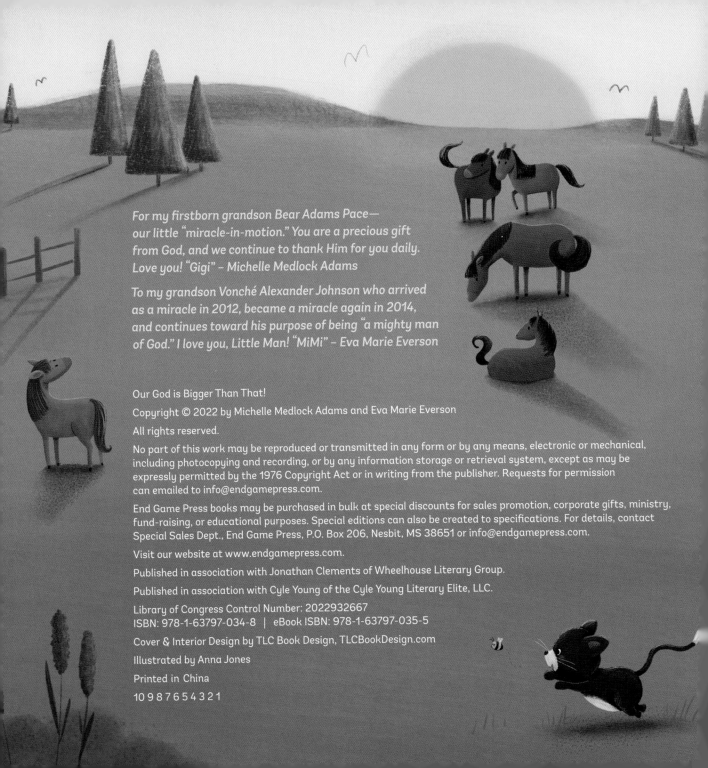

For my firstborn grandson Bear Adams Pace—
our little "miracle-in-motion." You are a precious gift
from God, and we continue to thank Him for you daily.
Love you! "Gigi" – Michelle Medlock Adams

To my grandson Vonché Alexander Johnson who arrived
as a miracle in 2012, became a miracle again in 2014,
and continues toward his purpose of being "a mighty man
of God." I love you, Little Man! "MiMi" – Eva Marie Everson

Our God is Bigger Than That!

Copyright © 2022 by Michelle Medlock Adams and Eva Marie Everson

All rights reserved.

No part of this work may be reproduced or transmitted in any form or by any means, electronic or mechanical, including photocopying and recording, or by any information storage or retrieval system, except as may be expressly permitted by the 1976 Copyright Act or in writing from the publisher. Requests for permission can emailed to info@endgamepress.com.

End Game Press books may be purchased in bulk at special discounts for sales promotion, corporate gifts, ministry, fund-raising, or educational purposes. Special editions can also be created to specifications. For details, contact Special Sales Dept., End Game Press, P.O. Box 206, Nesbit, MS 38651 or info@endgamepress.com.

Visit our website at www.endgamepress.com.

Published in association with Jonathan Clements of Wheelhouse Literary Group.

Published in association with Cyle Young of the Cyle Young Literary Elite, LLC.

Library of Congress Control Number: 2022932667
ISBN: 978-1-63797-034-8 | eBook ISBN: 978-1-63797-035-5

Cover & Interior Design by TLC Book Design, TLCBookDesign.com

Illustrated by Anna Jones

Printed in China

10 9 8 7 6 5 4 3 2 1

The Story Behind the Story
A Note from Michelle

This declaration, "Our God is bigger than that," became my battle cry when my oldest daughter, Abby, was diagnosed with HELLP syndrome in the final trimester of her pregnancy with our first grandchild. She delivered baby Bear a month early, with serious complications. Abby was admitted to ICU as the medical staff tried to find the source of her blood loss, and my newborn grandson was rushed to the NICU where he faced his own battles. Meanwhile, my sweet mother-in-law Martha was fighting for her life at a hospital four hours away with my husband by her side. It all seemed too much as I collapsed in the hospital hallway that August day in 2017. I called my close writer friend Eva Marie, who had been a nurse for many years, and asked her to explain all of the medical terms being thrown around. One by one, I told her the doctors' concerns regarding Abby, Bear, and Martha, and then I shared all of my greatest fears. Eva listened and then softly said, "I'm not going to lie to you. These are some big obstacles, but our God is bigger. He is bigger than all of that."

Her words filled my heart with hope and courage, and "Our God is bigger than that" became the battle cry for my whole family. Abby was able to go home to heal after two weeks in the hospital, and Bear joined her after another week. And my sweet mother-in-law went home to heaven the following month. Eighteen months later, Bear was diagnosed with a small tumor on the base of his brainstem, and we continue to declare: "Our God is bigger than that!" as we stand courageously with our grandson.

It's our hope that whatever you are facing today, that you'll grab hold of our declaration, "Our God is bigger than that!" and face your fears head on. We stand with you.

The sun comes up. The rooster crows.

The coffee starts to perk.

The farmer says, "Good morning, Dog.

It's time to go to work."

With that, the farmer and his dog

Walk through the morning dew.

Dog shivers at the cool wet grass.

A kitten shivers, too.

"I'm scared," says Kitten to her mom.
"The dog might see me here."
"Don't be afraid," her mama says.
"God's bigger than your fear.

"God's greater than your greatest fear.
He knows just where you're at.
No matter what you face in life—
Our God is bigger than that!"

The farmer calls, "Here, Chick, Chick, Chick!"
But one chick says, "No way!
I'm scared a fox might eat me up!
I'll hide here in the hay."

"Don't be afraid," says Mama Hen.
"No foxes are in sight.
Besides, God watches over us—
On call both day and night!

"God's greater than your greatest fear.
He knows just where you're at.
No matter what you face in life—
Our God is bigger than that!"

The farmer fills the trough with grain.

It's time to feed the cows.

Just then a mama mouse appears.

"I'll be back," Mama vows.

A little mouselet stays behind.

She crouches way down low.

"That cat might eat me,"
Mouselet says.

"I'm too afraid to go."

"Don't be afraid," says Mama Mouse.
"God's looking out for you.
He'll always be right by your side.
There's nothing He won't do.

"God's greater than your greatest fear.
He knows just where you're at.
No matter what you face in life—
Our God is bigger than that!"

The farmer calls the herd of cows.

But one calf will not come.

"I'm scared of biting flies,"
Calf says.

"One bit me on my bum!"

"Don't be afraid," says Mama Cow.
"I'll keep the flies away.
And even if I'm not around,
God's with you every day!

"God's greater than your greatest fear.
He knows just where you're at.
No matter what you face in life—
Our God is bigger than that!"

"Let's feed the horses,"
Farmer says.

But Dog won't budge at all.

"They cannot kick you,"
Farmer says.

"Each horse is in its stall."

Dog whines and whines. He's still afraid.

So Farmer picks him up.

"You'll be okay," the farmer says.

"I've got you—you're my pup.

"God's greater than your greatest fear.
He knows just where you're at.
No matter what you face in life—
Our God is bigger than that!"

It's been a very busy day.
The work is never done.
The farmer and his dog relax
And watch the sinking sun.

Inside, the farmer's little girl
Is snugly tucked in bed.
He comes inside to say goodnight
And kisses her sweet head.

"But, Daddy, I'm afraid," she says.
"It's way too dark in here!"
The farmer strokes his daughter's hair.
"I don't want you to fear."

"God's greater than your greatest fear.

He knows just where you're at.

No matter what you face in life—

Our God is bigger than that!"

A Note From the Authors to Parents

In the story of David and Goliath (1 Samuel 17), the Philistine giant brought fear to the Israelite army, yet David approached him boldly with just a few stones and a slingshot. That's because David knew that his God was bigger—bigger than his fears and bigger than Goliath.

Truth is, we are all afraid of something—all of us, children and adults. Just as we, as adults, do not want someone laughing at our fears, a child's fears should not be discounted but discussed in a nonjudgmental and accepting way.

We have addressed several fears, some natural and some imagined, in this book. For example, the kitten is afraid of her "natural enemy" (the dog), but most of us know of households with dogs and cats who not only get along, they enjoy playing together. We also feature healthy fears in this book. For example, the chick fears the fox, and the mouselet fears the cat. In real life, we should have a healthy fear of natural predators and dangerous situations. But we can't let those fears—even the healthy ones—stop us from living our lives. These are topics you may wish to discuss with your child.

We also wanted to show fear of the "physical." A kick from a horse hurts, of course. But there are ways to approach horses to keep from getting kicked. Once we learn that, we no longer have to be afraid.

Many children are afraid of the dark or things that "go bump in the night." Reassuring your child that you are close by (and perhaps a nightlight) can ease that common fear.

Finally, we wished to show that when children are afraid, and that fear brings them to tears, they can come to a parent for protection and guidance and comfort.

So, yes. It's okay to be afraid. *Our God is Bigger Than That* reminds our children (and us) not to let fear get so big, it stops them (and us) from doing the things we enjoy. Remember: God is bigger than your greatest fear! He can handle it!

Each animal in the text (and the farmer's little girl) faced their fears, which we all must do. And that can be a scary thing! Teaching your children that God goes with them everywhere (Matthew 28:20) and He promises never to leave them (Joshua 1:5) will help diminish those fears.

So say this out loud with your child: no fear here! Our God is bigger than that!

Blessings on your household,
Michelle Medlock Adams & Eva Marie Everson